Peppa's Magical Unicorn

Adapted by Lauren Holloway and Cala Spinner

This book is based on the TV series *Peppa Pig*. *Peppa Pig* is created by Neville Astley and Mark Baker.
Peppa Pig © Astley Baker Davies Ltd/Entertainment One UK Ltd 2003.

ISBN 978-1-338-58400-4

10 9 8 7 6 5 4 3 2 1   20 21 22 23 24
Printed in the U.S.A.   40

First printing 2020
Book design by Mercedes Padró

www.peppapig.com

SCHOLASTIC INC.

One rainy day, Peppa introduces Suzy to her toy horse.

"This is Horsey Twinkle Toes," Peppa says.
"It's very nice to meet you, Miss Twinkle Toes,"
Suzy replies.

Peppa gallops up to her room while riding
Horsey Twinkle Toes.
"Giddyup!" Peppa shouts while Suzy watches.

Downstairs, Daddy Pig hears a lot of noise.
He comes up to see what is going on.
"We're playing horses," Peppa explains.
Daddy Pig sees that *Peppa* is playing horses.
Suzy is sitting quietly.

"Do you think it's Suzy's turn to play, Peppa?"
asks Daddy Pig.
"Yes," Peppa replies.
But Suzy says she doesn't want to play horses.
She wants to play *unicorns*!

"Well, Horsey Twinkle Toes is a magic horse," Peppa replies. "She can be a unicorn whenever she feels like it." Suzy is still disappointed.
"Unicorns have rainbow tails," says Suzy.
Horsey Twinkle Toes does not have a rainbow tail.

That gives Peppa an idea. They put colorful ribbons in Horsey Twinkle Toes's tail!

But Suzy is still disappointed.
"I wish Horsey Twinkle Toes was a real unicorn,"
says Suzy.
"And I wish she was really, really, really sparkly!"
adds Peppa.

Daddy Pig brings a tray of cookies and juice out to
Peppa, Suzy, and Horsey Twinkle Toes.
"Who would like to hear a bedtime story?" he asks.

"Please, can you read us a bedtime story about unicorns, Daddy?" asks Peppa.
"Of course," Daddy Pig replies. "Once upon a time, there was a unicorn that came to life!"
"Wow!" Suzy says. "I wish Horsey Twinkle Toes would do that."

That gives Daddy Pig an idea.
"Why don't you build Horsey Twinkle Toes a place to sleep in?" he asks.
Peppa and Suzy are excited! They put together the coziest place for Horsey Twinkle Toes to sleep.

But it is so cozy, they fall asleep in it too!

While Peppa and Suzy sleep, Daddy Pig picks up Horsey Twinkle Toes, tiptoes outside, and starts to paint . . .

He paints some more . . .

Then glues . . .

And glues some more . . .

It takes Daddy Pig all night, but finally,
he adds the final touch—a horn!
"Ta-da!" Daddy Pig whispers.

Then he returns Horsey Twinkle Toes
to Suzy and Peppa.

In the morning, Peppa and Suzy wake up.
"Wow!" they gasp loudly and hug each other.

Horsey Twinkle Toes has transformed into a
magical unicorn!

Peppa, Suzy, George, Mummy and Daddy Pig all sit down for breakfast.
Peppa tells her family all about Horsey Twinkle Toes.

Snore!
Snore!

"How wonderful!" says Mummy Pig. "It sounds like you and Suzy have had the perfect sleepover."
"Yes!" replies Peppa. "But why is Daddy so sleepy?"
Daddy Pig can't answer. He is snoring!

After breakfast, Peppa and Suzy play with Horsey
Twinkle Toes outside.
"I love your magical unicorn!" cheers Suzy.
"Me too," says Peppa.
Everyone loves magical unicorns! Especially Daddy Pig!

Snore!
Snore!